THE HUNCHBACK
OF NOTRE-DAME

A DK PUBLISHING BOOK

A RETELLING OF VICTOR HUGO'S *Notre-Dame de Paris* FOR YOUNG READERS

Editor Natascha Biebow
Senior Editor Marie Greenwood
Series Art Editor Jane Thomas
Production Katy Holmes
Managing Art Editor Chris Fraser
Picture Research Louise Thomas and Elizabeth Bacon
DTP Designer Kim Browne

For Elissa and the Wednesday evening gang – JS

First American Edition, 1997
2 4 6 8 10 9 7 5 3 1

Published in the United States by DK Publishing, Inc.
95 Madison Avenue, New York, New York 10016
Visit us on the World Wide Web at http://www.dk.com

Published in Great Britain by Dorling Kindersley Ltd.

A catalog record for this book is available from the Library of Congress.

ISBN 0-7894-1491-0

Color reproduction by Bright Arts in Hong Kong
Printed by Graphicom in Italy

THE HUNCHBACK OF NOTRE-DAME

VICTOR HUGO

Retold by JIMMY SYMONDS

Illustrated by
TONY SMITH

CONTENTS

Quasimodo

Claude Frollo

Esmeralda

Djali

Gringoire

INTRODUCTION

*T*he *Hunchback of Notre-Dame* has become something of a fairy tale. The story has been turned into a movie, an opera, even a cartoon.

The original book was published in France in 1831 under the title *Notre-Dame de Paris*, and it was not a fairy tale. Nor was it about the hunchback (only when the story was translated into English in 1833 did the hunchback get into the title). It was an adult historical novel written to make people aware of the need to preserve the great cathedral of Notre-Dame, which had been at the heart of an earlier society – medieval Paris. Victor Hugo described a colorful mix of people from the lowliest beggars and gypsies to the king and the aristocracy. This was a society of dreadful injustice, in which torture and hangings were everyday occurrences. But it was also a society in which an orphaned, crippled hunchback could be brought up to be the bellringer of the great Notre-Dame Cathedral.

Quasimodo has become the memorable focus of this sad tale of love and longing. Adopted at birth by Claude Frollo, the Archdeacon of Notre-Dame, the hunchback becomes devoted to the gypsy dancer, Esmeralda. They get caught up in a web of intrigue involving Esmeralda's other admirers, not knowing that their fates had been destined to be entwined at birth.

Victor Hugo devotes much of his novel to descriptions of medieval Paris, especially the majestic cathedral towering over the boat-shaped *Île de la Cité* in the middle of the Seine River. Here are the glorious rose-windows, the Gothic towers, the intricately carved portals, and the grotesque gargoyles.

This *Eyewitness Classic* edition of the novel shows the medieval Paris that Hugo describes, using engravings, illustrations, and photographs. A sensitive retelling, it brings clarity to a complex plot, while keeping the essence of Hugo's compelling original.

Captain Phoebus

Fleur-de-Lys

The recluse

Jehan

Clopin Trouillefou

Medieval Paris

The story of *The Hunchback of Notre-Dame* is set in 1482 in Paris, the capital of France. The action takes place in and around Notre-Dame Cathedral on the Île de la Cité, the "island of the city," that stands at the center of Paris in the middle of the Seine River.

Paris seal

BEGINNINGS OF PARIS

Paris began on the Île de la Cité as a small fishing village. In 53 BC, the Romans conquered it. Then, in AD 357, invaders from the north renamed the city Paris.

By 1482, Paris was the capital of France and 25 times the size of the Roman village. More than 200,000 people lived there. Houses and markets had sprung up on both banks of the Seine.

Roman remains at the Cluny Museum in Paris

THE SEINE RIVER

Notre-Dame Cathedral stood along the Seine River, the most important thoroughfare in medieval Paris. People used the river to travel from one side of town to another, and to transport goods from as far away as Italy and the Netherlands. The river also powered the grain mills along its banks.

The Île de la Cité is shaped like a ship.

Fortified wall

Water supply

Water for drinking, washing, and cooking was pumped from the Seine to public fountains. As Paris grew, the demand for water became too great for the fountains, so people bought extra supplies from watersellers.

Boat travel

Boatmen used long poles to paddle along the river, transporting people, animals, and goods such as vegetables, fish, wood, wine, and salt into Paris.

The Île de la Cité

Two main buildings stood on the Île de la Cité: Notre-Dame Cathedral and the Palace of Justice. This made the island the center of government and religion in Paris, and a focal point for the action of *The Hunchback of Notre-Dame*.

Court of Miracles

Some of Paris's outcasts pretended to be blind or maimed so people would give them money. They lived in a square nicknamed the Court of Miracles, where they "miraculously" recovered each night.

Tall, pointed turrets lined the Parisian skyline.

Town walls

The walls of Paris were 8 ft (2.5 m) thick, with 25 gates and as many as 500 towers.

Notre-Dame Cathedral

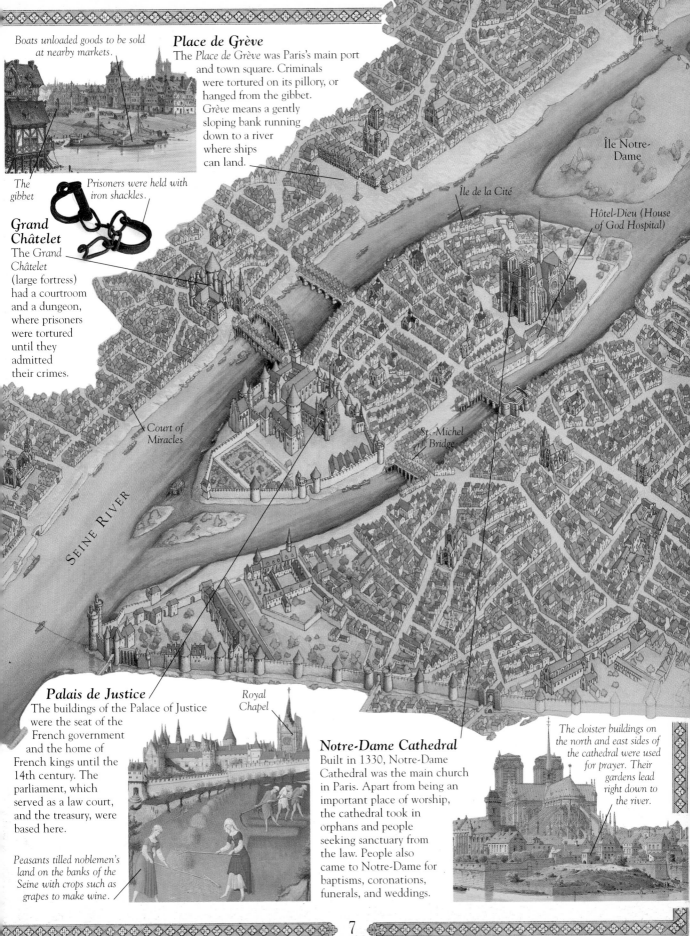

Place de Grève

The *Place de Grève* was Paris's main port and town square. Criminals were tortured on its pillory, or hanged from the gibbet. *Grève* means a gently sloping bank running down to a river where ships can land.

Boats unloaded goods to be sold at nearby markets.

The gibbet

Prisoners were held with iron shackles.

Grand Châtelet

The *Grand Châtelet* (large fortress) had a courtroom and a dungeon, where prisoners were tortured until they admitted their crimes.

Court of Miracles

Île Notre-Dame

Île de la Cité

Hôtel-Dieu (House of God Hospital)

St.-Michel Bridge

SEINE RIVER

Palais de Justice

The buildings of the Palace of Justice were the seat of the French government and the home of French kings until the 14th century. The parliament, which served as a law court, and the treasury, were based here.

Peasants tilled noblemen's land on the banks of the Seine with crops such as grapes to make wine.

Royal Chapel

Notre-Dame Cathedral

Built in 1330, Notre-Dame Cathedral was the main church in Paris. Apart from being an important place of worship, the cathedral took in orphans and people seeking sanctuary from the law. People also came to Notre-Dame for baptisms, coronations, funerals, and weddings.

The cloister buildings on the north and east sides of the cathedral were used for prayer. Their gardens lead right down to the river.

PEOPLE OF PARIS

The characters in the story come from all the different levels of society in medieval Paris, from the very rich to the very poor. Wealthy noblemen and clergymen pass gypsies and outcasts on the foul-smelling streets of the *Île de la Cité* and the *Place de Grève* every day.

Most medieval houses had two floors, and were made from wood and stone. Those who could afford them had slate roofs, which lasted longer than thatched ones.

PARISIAN SOCIETY

Everyone from the king to the lowliest peasant met on the streets of Paris in 1482.

The King
King Louis XI ruled France at the time of the story. When he was in Paris, he attended daily mass at Notre-Dame Cathedral.

King Louis XI ruled France from 1461–83.

Nobles
Noblemen were rich landowners. They advised the king in government and defended France at war. Noblewomen were in charge of running their households.

Nobleman

Noble-woman

Merchants
Merchants brought goods such as food, clothing, and furniture to trade in the markets of Paris. They often trained young people in their trade as apprentices.

Peasant
Peasants worked the land for the Parisian nobles in return for basic food and protection.

Wealthy home
Nobles lived in large houses, often called *hôtels*, with separate rooms for bathing, cooking, eating, sleeping, and socializing. This scene shows some nobles at dinner with their guests.

A noblewoman watching the hustle and bustle below.

Merchants lived and worked in the same house. On the ground floor, they had a shop or workroom, while the upstairs room was used as a kitchen, bedroom, and hall. The scissors hanging in front of this shop show that it belongs to a tailor.

Animals such as chickens and dogs roamed the streets freely, but King Louis VI had outlawed pigs from the streets of Paris in the 12th century.

A well-dressed nobleman

A tailor helped noblemen choose cloth for new outfits.

There were no sewers, so foul-smelling waste accumulated in the street gutter.

Going to market
Weekly markets were held in medieval Paris. Peasants driving cattle, sheep, pigs, and chicken all came. Merchants' stalls sold goods such as cheese, eggs, salt, pots and pans, tools, knives, shoes, and cloth.

Merchants stopped on the streets to exchange ideas.

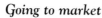

Towers of Notre-Dame Cathedral

THE CHURCH

Most people in medieval Europe believed in the same religion – Christianity. The Church had its own laws, lands, and taxes, which made it powerful.

Pope Sixtus IV was Pope in 1482.

Archdeacon
Every cathedral had an archdeacon, who said mass, and supervised the distribution of alms to the poor and needy.

Pope
The Pope in Rome was the head of the Church. He was "God's messenger on Earth," and had as much power as the king.

Chamber pots were emptied out of windows with cries of "Look out, water!"

Since few people could read, merchants hung out signs with symbols, such as these beer barrels for a tavern.

Officer
Paris had no real police force. Officers from the king's bodyguard and groups of noblemen patrolled the streets to keep order.

Men gathered in taverns to meet friends, and play card or dice games. Since water was dirty and diseased, most people drank wine or beer.

Students
When they weren't in class, students had fun in the tavern.

SOCIAL OUTCASTS

Beggars, gypsies, and people with disabilities were the outcasts of Parisian society. Most were poor and homeless, and people saw them as a threat.

Gypsies
Gypsies were nomads, who traveled from city to city. Some earned a living by entertaining people in the streets.

The hunchback was an outcast.

People carried their purchases in baskets.

Officers made arrests.

Gypsy dancers made a living by entertaining people passing by.

Busy streets were ideal places for pickpockets to work.

Beggars and vagabonds
There were many poor and homeless people in Paris. Some of these outcasts begged for money; others worked as pickpockets and thieves.

Prologue

THE BELLRINGER OF NOTRE-DAME

Notre-Dame Cathedral today

Notre-Dame Cathedral
At the time of this story, Notre-Dame Cathedral looked much the same as it does today, except that it had eleven steps leading to the door. Notre-Dame means Our Lady.

Notre-Dame's medieval steps

Foundlings
Babies who were deformed or born to unmarried parents were often abandoned on the steps of Notre-Dame. Priests gave them to kind people to care for. In 1552, an orphanage was built nearby.

Foundlings were left outside orphanages in later times.

ONE SPRING DAY IN PARIS IN 1467, four old women huddled outside the steps of Notre-Dame Cathedral. They were looking at the abandoned babies lying there on a bed of wooden planks, waiting to be saved. Warm sun shone on the orphans' faces but it did not stop them from crying. The women were staring at one child in particular.

"That's no baby! It's a monkey gone wrong!"

"It's the work of the devil!"

The child lay squealing on the wooden bed, one eye peering out at the women. Its deformed head was surrounded by thick, red hair.

"I'd rather nurse a vampire! Look at that wart on its face!"

"That's no wart. It's an egg with more monsters in it!"

A wealthy lady leaving the cathedral after morning prayers with her daughter stopped and looked at the wooden bed in amazement.

"Really! I thought they only left humans here!" she exclaimed as she passed by. She dropped a coin into the copper alms bowl, and hurried away.

"Nobody shall ever look after that revolting creature!" exclaimed one woman.

"I shall!" said a voice.

The women looked up and saw a young priest gather up the child into his cassock and hurry into the gloomy darkness of the cathedral.

"That was Claude Frollo!" exclaimed one woman. "I told you he was a sorcerer!"

Quasimodo howled with glee, as he swung on the big bell.

But Frollo didn't hear. He was anxious to baptize the one-eyed hunchbacked crooked-kneed creature that he had just adopted.

"Today is Quasimodo Sunday so I will call you 'Quasimodo'!"

He looked with compassion at the poor, deformed child and vowed to bring him up as if he were his brother.

And so he did. He taught Quasimodo to talk and read and write. And when Frollo became the Archdeacon of Notre-Dame, Quasimodo became the bellringer. Hidden from the outside world, the cathedral became his universe. Here, the marble statues and stone monsters did not laugh at his ugly face, but stared down kindly instead.

The bells became his best friends, and nothing could match the excitement he felt when he rang the big bell. He would leap onto it, grasp it between his knees, and shout with joy as he felt it vibrate through his whole body. But sadly, it was these beloved bells that made Quasimodo go deaf.

Quasimodo
The holy day of Quasimodo fell on the first Sunday after Easter. The Latin words quasi modo *were the first words sung in church at mass on this day.*

Medieval Latin Bible

Baptizing the baby
Babies were brought to their local church to be baptized The priest sprinkled holy water on the baby's head and said a prayer to make it a Christian.

Baptizing ceremony

Ringing the bells
Bells were important to every medieval town. They called people to Mass, told them the time, and warned them when enemies neared city gates. Bellringers were in charge of "spreading the news," whether mourning a death or celebrating a wedding.

Three Wise Men

Epiphany

The Feast of Epiphany, held on the 6th of January, is one of the oldest festival days celebrated by the Christian Church. It marks the visit of the Three Wise Men to the baby Jesus.

Feast of Fools

In this Christian festival, the faithful elected their own pope. He pretended to be the head of the Church for a day, and put on a mock tiara. He was then carried through the streets of Paris.

Pope's jeweled tiara

Medieval mysteries

Mystery plays, loosely based on stories from the Bible, were performed on feast days. Large crowds jostled to see actors mock soldiers, judges, doctors, and even priests.

Chapter one

FEAST DAY

CLAUDE FROLLO had a real little brother named Jehan, whom he loved dearly. In 1482, when Frollo was the archdeacon, and Quasimodo was the bellringer of Notre-Dame, Jehan was a student – though not a very serious one.

On the sixth of January, along with most of the people of Paris, Jehan was enjoying the double holiday of the Feast of

"Yoo-hoo!" shouted the crowd. "Start the play!"

Epiphany and the Feast of Fools. A huge crowd had gathered in the Great Hall of the Palace of Justice to watch a mystery play. Jehan climbed a column to get a good view.

"They say it's about a golden dolphin . . ." whispered an old lady.

"Hurry up," yelled Jehan. "It's freezing cold! We need warming up with a good story!"

"Quiet! It's about to begin!"

But nothing happened.

"Uh . . . we must wait for the Ambassadors," replied Gringoire, the author of the play.

A beggar jumped onto the stage to show the crowd the many sores on his legs.

"Get him off!" exclaimed Gringoire.

"That's Clopin, King of the Outcasts!" shouted Jehan. "He was limping with the other leg yesterday!"

He hurled a coin into Clopin's greasy hat.

"The play!" chanted the crowd.

"I know," came a voice from the crowd. "While we're waiting for the play to begin, let's choose a fools' pope like they do in my town!"

The crowd roared its approval.

The Royal Chapel across from the stage had a broken rose window.

"Put your heads through that hole! Whoever has the ugliest face will be crowned! Who will be the first?"

A kaleidoscope of different faces appeared.

"Ugly?" cried Clopin, counting his money. "My mother was uglier without even trying!"

Now a face appeared like no other . . . one-eyed, a mouth the shape of a twisted horseshoe, and teeth like castle battlements.

"What a monster!"

"It's Quasimodo, my brother's bellringer!" called Jehan.

"Look at his hunched back!"

"Yes, he shall be our fools' pope!"

The crowd placed a cardboard tiara on Quasimodo's head, lifted him above their heads, and carried him out into the streets, cheering and waving.

Someone said, "He doesn't know what's going on. He's deaf."

"He may be deaf," said Jehan, "but he's not dumb."

"What about my play?" moaned Gringoire.

But the actors had followed Quasimodo out onto the cold streets of Paris.

Great Hall | Dungeon | Royal Chapel

Palace of Justice
This was home to the French kings until the 14th century. Its many buildings included the Royal Chapel, the king's apartments, the dungeon, and the royal gardens.

Great Hall
In 1482, the Great Hall was the largest covered meeting place in the world. It was used for royal audiences, banquets, and feast day celebrations.

Detail from a rose window in the Sainte-Chapelle

Royal Chapel
The entire Palace was lavishly decorated. The king's place of worship, the Sainte-Chapelle, had a splendid rose window above the door, with 86 stained-glass panels.

"Quasimodo for fools' pope!" cried the people.

People were hanged from the gibbet.

Town square
The Place de Grève *was the only town square in Paris in 1482. The side bordering the river led onto the quay of a bustling port, and the gibbet at the center of the square was frequently used for punishments and executions.*

On the move
For centuries gypsies traveled from place to place, making their living by selling their crafts and helping with farmwork. Caravans, such as this 19th-century one, were home to many gypsies all year round.

Persian rugs were highly prized for their texture and patterns.

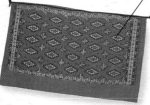

Intricate carpets
Gypsies brought handmade Persian (Iranian) rugs with them on their travels from Asia to Europe.

Chapter two

ESMERALDA

A pretty little white goat watched its mistress dance.

GRINGOIRE LEFT THE EMPTY PALACE and walked alone through the dark streets of Paris, where the cold wind reminded him it was still deep winter. His wanderings took him over a bridge to the *Place de Grève*. Here, a huge crowd had gathered around a gypsy girl, dancing on a brightly colored Persian rug to the rattle of a tambourine. A little goat with a snowy-white coat

stood near the gypsy, whose exquisite beauty made Gringoire instantly forget the heartache of his disastrous play.

"Who's the girl?" he asked.

"Have you never heard of Esmeralda?" came the astonished reply.

Gringoire made his way nearer to her, brushing his way past a tall man in a dark cloak who seemed to be particularly fascinated by the

young girl's ability to dance and charm.

"Surely," whispered Gringoire, "that's Jehan's brother, Claude Frollo, the Archdeacon of Notre-Dame! It's unlike him to leave the cathedral."

Esmeralda stopped dancing, kneeled on the colorful rug, and held the tambourine out to her goat.

"Djali," said the dancer, "what month of the year are we in?"

The goat raised a front hoof and hit the tambourine once. The crowd applauded.

"Djali, what day of January is it?"

The white goat looked into the eyes of the gypsy and tapped the tambourine six times.

"Bravo!" cheered the crowd.

"Now, my darling Djali," continued Esmeralda, "what hour of the day is it?"

The goat tapped seven times just as the bells of Notre-Dame Cathedral chimed seven o'clock. Cheers rang out of the crowd, but the man in black said, "There's witchcraft at work."

Then the noise of the crowd was drowned by the noise of a strange procession. It was the fools' pope, followed by rogues and thieves. Quasimodo bowed and lowered his tiara to the crowds. He did not realize they were laughing at him. Instead, he smiled through his broken teeth.

Then, suddenly, the man in the black cloak dashed out of the crowd, snatched Quasimodo's cardboard tiara from his head, and threw it violently onto the cobblestones.

"You are making a fool of yourself!" he yelled.

Quasimodo jumped down off of the throne and kneeled humbly before the man in black. It was indeed Frollo.

Goats quickly learn to balance.

Clever goat tricks
Gypsies have a rich tradition in entertainment and dance. Many kept performing animals. Goats were popular because they learned tricks easily.

Animal-skin tambourine

Street performers
Gypsies learned tunes from all over the world, which they played in public squares to earn a living. Women often danced to the beat of a tambourine.

Quasimodo kneeled fearfully on the cobblestones at Frollo's feet.

15

KEEPING ORDER IN PARIS

Dangerous backstreets
Paris's narrow, badly lit alleys were perilous places. Thieves and murderers could easily hide here in the dark shadows.

In charge
The king at the time of this story was King Louis XI (1461–83). He appointed a new provost in 1461, whose job was to keep order in Paris.

King's bodyguard
The provost appointed the captain of the king's bodyguard to patrol the dark streets of Paris with a squadron of archers. They wore brigandine armor for protection.

Brigandine armor was made of metal plates sewn onto cloth or leather.

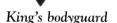

Frollo made Quasimodo follow him down a dark alley.

"This all seems quite remarkable," observed Gringoire, "but it doesn't stop me from being cold, hungry, penniless, and with nowhere to lay my head tonight!"

He watched Esmeralda as she collected the coins from the rug before folding it carefully, placing it under her arm, and walking away with Djali.

"I think I may be a little in love with her," he thought. "Perhaps I'll follow her and see where she goes. I have nothing else to do . . ."

Deeper and deeper into the maze of dark streets she went until Gringoire heard a scream. He saw Esmeralda lifted up like a silken scarf onto the shoulders of a creature with a hunched back. Another man in a black cloak stood by them.

"Why, that's Quasimodo and . . . surely, it can't be the priest!"

"Murder!" cried Esmeralda.

Passing soldiers from the king's bodyguard heard her call, and released her from the hunchback's clutches. The other man disappeared.

Quasimodo roared and foamed.

"Hold him, men!" shouted the captain.

Esmeralda looked up into the captain's eyes as he lifted her gently onto his horse.

"My name is Phoebus, sweet angel. I'm glad we were passing!"

She blushed deep crimson.

"Thank you for saving me!" she said. Then she slid down from his horse and ran off.

"The dove has flown away," Phoebus whispered, "but the bat remains. Take him away! Beat him if he bites!" he called to his soldiers.

Gringoire watched as the soldiers bound Quasimodo's hands together, then rode off on their horses.

The poet walked on alone toward the saddest corner of the city, where the flames of street fires danced on the walls of

crumbling houses, and the homeless huddled
together to keep each other warm.

"Where will I sleep? What will I eat?"

The poor swarmed around him like flies.

"Money . . ."

"But I have nothing!" cried Gringoire.
"I am only a poor poet."

But they crept around him like spiders.

"Take him to King Clopin!"

Gringoire was dragged through a
stinking doorway and into a vast
courtyard lit by a large, crackling
fire. When he looked
around him, the
poet realized he
was in the Court
of Miracles, the
home of Paris'
outcasts. And there,
towering above him,
stood their king,
Clopin Trouillefou.

*Two archers of the
king's bodyguard
seized Quasimodo.*

Time to light up
*There were no streetlights in
Paris at this time. Residents
were supposed to put lighted
candles in their windows
at nightfall.*

17

Chapter three
COURT OF MIRACLES

COURT OF MIRACLES
The Court of Miracles was a city square, home to thieves, gypsies, and beggars – the outcasts of Paris. Not even the night watchmen dared to enter its filthy, unpaved courtyard.

Balancing carefully, Gringoire reached toward the dummy.

CLOPIN, KING OF THE OUTCASTS, sat on a broken barrel stuffed with stinking straw, holding a leather whip. A rat scuttled across the filthy cobblestones.

"Bow when you are brought to my throne!" he yelled.

"Ah . . . What throne?" questioned Gringoire.

"You are in my Court of Miracles!" said Clopin, as he hurled his crown of rags at him. "I think we shall hang you. It might be fun!"

"No! You can't!" Gringoire thought quickly. "I am a poet!"

"A poet! Then we shall hang you immediately! I hate poets. Only this morning I was bored to tears by a play that didn't even begin!"

Gringoire shuddered.

"Where is my crown?" asked King Clopin.

"Here, your majesty!" said a woman with boils on her arms.

"Hang him!" said Clopin. "No, wait! We'll give him a chance . . ."

Gringoire's heart leaped with hope.

Clopin pointed to a dummy hanging above a three-legged stool nearby. "If you can stand on tiptoe on that stool and take the wallet from the dummy's pocket without making the bells jangle, you are free to go."

"But what if the wind blows the bells?" asked Gringoire, timidly.

"You'll hang!"

Nervously, Gringoire lifted himself onto the toe of his left foot, his hand shaking like a tree in a storm. He touched the dummy, then lost his balance. One hundred bells tinkled sweetly in the night air.

"Hang him!" cried the ragamuffins.

Clopin stood up from his throne. "Wait! I am feeling kind. If any of you disgusting creatures will marry him, he will be spared!"

A hag with vile breath stepped forward. "Do you have any other shoes without holes, pretty one?" she asked.

Gringoire looked down. "I am a poet. I don't need good shoes." She spat on him and stormed away.

"Anyone else?" cried Clopin. "I'll count up to three. One, two . . ."

"I'll take him!"

Gringoire looked up, expecting a monster, but it was Esmeralda.

"Perhaps I have reached heaven, for here is my angel!" he whispered to himself.

"Blast!" spat Clopin. "I was looking forward to a good hanging!"

King Clopin dropped a clay jug on the ground. It smashed into four large pieces. "You shall have to stay married to him for four years!"

"Very well," replied the gypsy, "but I only married him to save him from being hanged." And she disappeared off with Gringoire to her room.

King of the outcasts
The most popular and skillful of the outcasts was elected to be their leader and protector.

Playing outcasts
Many outcasts pretended to be sick or injured so people would pity them and give them money.

Miracle cures
Every night, these outcasts were miraculously transformed in their court. They took off their false bandages, and could walk and see again.

Stealing from the rich
Some outcasts also worked as pickpockets and thieves in busy marketplaces, where they would not get caught.

Chapter four

Quasimodo's punishment

O N THE DAY AFTER THE FEAST DAY, Quasimodo was put on trial. The courtroom at the *Grand Châtelet* was packed to the rafters, for everybody had heard how the fools' pope had tried to steal a gypsy dancer. The court clerk was already in his place at the table covered in *fleur-de-lys*, next to the big armchair of carved oak.

This was the most important seat in the courtroom,

Grand Châtelet
The Grand Châtelet stood oacross from the Palace of Justice on the other side of the Seine River. It was used as a courtroom and a dungeon.

French
kings' coat
of arms

Royal emblem
The fleur-de-lys, or "flower of the lily," was used in the French kings' coat of arms. This decorative symbol appeared on all official items, such as tapestries in courtrooms, seals on letters, on flags, and on royal uniforms.

Flower of
the lily

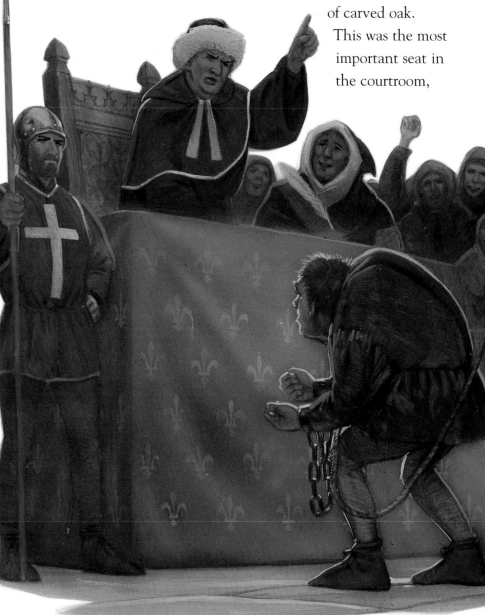

"Do you plead guilty or not guilty?" the judge asked Quasimodo loudly.

Provost   The public

and it belonged to the provost, who acted as the trial judge.

The provost was late and in a bad mood. He entered coughing and spluttering from the cold. "Silence in court!" he ordered in a very loud voice so no one would guess that he was deaf. He shuffled his papers and looked up.

"What is your name?" he asked Quasimodo, who stood shackled before him, heavily guarded by the court sergeants.

But, thanks to the bells of Notre-Dame, Quasimodo was also deaf. So he had absolutely no idea that the judge had spoken to him. And the judge continued to ask questions, not knowing that Quasimodo had not even answered his first one:

"Good. Your age?"

Silence. The judge nodded.

"Now, your trade?"

Silence again. The audience began to whisper.

The judge assumed Quasimodo had replied and continued, "You are charged with disturbing the peace and trying to steal a young girl against her will. Do you plead 'guilty' or 'not guilty'?" Silence.

"Clerk, have you written down what the defendant has said so far?"

At that, the crowd broke into roars of laughter at the two men who could see but not hear each other.

The judge lost his temper. "Are you making fun of me, you one-eyed rascal?" he yelled. "For your insolence you shall be put on the pillory at the *Place de Grève* and whipped until you learn the meaning of good behavior! Take him away!"

On trial   The accused
Apart from keeping order in Paris, the provost acted as judge. He heard cases where people were accused of crimes such as public disorder, theft, and witchcraft.

Court clerk

Keeping records
The court clerk wrote down everything that was said in court. At the end of the trial, he read out the sentence before the judge signed it.

The halberd's battle-ax could maim unruly prisoners.

Sturdy metal shackles

Shackling the accused
Court sergeants kept a firm hold on prisoners' shackled wrists, and tackled any resistance with their halberds.

21

Outside the courthouse, three women and a small boy carrying a maize cake gathered on the street. Festive ribbons, rags, feathers, and pearls of candlewax littered the ground.

"They're going to torture the ugly bellringer for stealing the gypsy!" said Oudarde.

"Let's go and watch!" replied Gervaise.

"Listen! It's the gypsy's tambourine!" remarked Oudarde.

"Oh, no! She'll steal my child," cried Mahiette, the woman with the boy, fearfully. "I don't want what happened to Paquette to happen to me."

"Who's Paquette?" asked Gervaise.

"What! Don't you know her sad little story?" replied Mahiette. "You shall hear it and then you'll know the reason I'm afraid of gypsies.

"Sixteen springs ago, there lived in Reims a poor but beautiful woman called Paquette la Chantefleurie. She had an exquisite baby daughter. Such was her love for the child she would kiss her a thousand times a day and only tie the richest pink ribbons in her hair.

"One day Paquette heard the gypsies were in town so she took her daughter to see them. They took Paquette's last penny, and told her that her daughter would grow up to be a beautiful princess.

"Paquette was so thrilled that she ran all the way home with her baby girl, put her to bed, and went to the houses of her friends telling them the good news.

"But when she returned home, her daughter was gone! All that remained was a pink baby shoe on the floor.

"Paquette wept and wailed and searched the streets of Reims every day.

"Then, one afternoon, she heard the cries of a

Three women stood gossiping, while the boy eyed the maize cake.

Maize cake
Maize cake, made of ground corn called meal, was cheap and filling.

Fortune-telling
For centuries gypsies were known for fortune-telling. Many people believed they could predict the future by looking into crystal balls.

"Paquette had a pretty baby girl."

Public breviary
*Breviaries (books of prayers
and psalms) were expensive
because they were copied out
by hand. They were kept on
stands in public places so
everyone could read them.*

Solitary cell
*Recluses are people who live
in solitude, often to mourn a
sudden death or to reach
spiritual purity through prayer
and reflection.*

child in her house. Her heart leaped with joy. She thought her prayers had been answered and that her beautiful daughter had been returned.

"But there, in her daughter's place, was the ugliest baby she had ever seen. It had one eye and thick red hair.

"Paquette had never seen such an ugly baby before!"

"Paquette thought she would go mad. She ran out into the street, screaming. There, she met a little boy, who told her that he had seen a gypsy woman coming down her stairs with a bundle in a white blanket.

"Paquette ran as fast as she could to the gypsy camp, but when she got there, the gypsies had gone and all that remained was a smoldering bonfire. In the ashes she saw a little pink ribbon.

"'Oh God!' wailed Paquette. 'They've burned my daughter! They've eaten her!'

"And she was never seen again," said Mahiette, finishing her story.

They were standing at the public breviary on the *Place de Grève*, in front of the Rat-hole. This dark cell was the home of a broken-hearted recluse.

"What a sad story!" exclaimed Gervaise. "No wonder you're scared of gypsies."

"And the funny thing is," continued Oudarde, "that the recluse in the Rat-hole is just as terrified of gypsies as you are."

"What happened to the ugly baby?" wondered Gervaise.

"The archbishop blessed it, and sent it to Paris to be left on the steps of Notre-Dame with all the other orphans."

Mahiette peered into the recluse's lonely cell, and let out a gasp. "It's her!" she exclaimed. "It's Paquette!"

The other women and the boy crowded around to look.

Shaking, the recluse cried, "Take that child away! The gypsy's going to come!"

"We've brought you some maize cake," said Mahiette, but the recluse turned away.

The recluse kneeled all alone in her dark cell.

Prisoners were "turned" on the pillory wheel for the crowd to see.

The neck and wrists were secured in the stocks.

Up to six people could be punished on this pillory.

At the pillory

Quasimodo was taken to a simple pillory – a wheel on a platform. Many other pillories had wooden frames with locks for as many as six prisoners' necks and their wrists.

Horrible torture

Crowds flocked to see criminals being whipped and tortured on the pillory. They laughed, and threw rotten eggs and vegetables as the prisoner was turned.

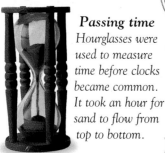

Passing time

Hourglasses were used to measure time before clocks became common. It took an hour for sand to flow from top to bottom.

Thirst quencher

Hollowed-out gourds were dried, filled with water, and hung around the waist.

The three women's attention was distracted by the awful cries of Quasimodo being dragged out from the courthouse.

"Look! They're taking him to the pillory now!"

An angry crowd, who had only the day before cheered the fools' pope, now jeered as the torturer stripped Quasimodo to the waist, and bound him to the pillory. An hourglass was turned over and placed before him.

"Watch the red sand, vile monster! Your beating will last one hour."

Through silent tears, Quasimodo watched the crowd holler and shout at him. "Your ugliness made my cat grow seven claws on one paw!"

The torturer stamped his foot, and the pillory wheel began to turn. Lashes hissed like snakes onto Quasimodo's bare back.

"Water," whispered Quasimodo.

"Here's water for you, beast!" shouted someone, throwing a dirty rag drenched with rain from the gutter at his face. A dead spider landed on his giant wart.

"My house fell down because you looked at it!"

"Water . . ." he cried, but the crowd threw only rags or insults.

Now Claude Frollo passed by the pillory, riding on a black mule. Quasimodo's heart beat faster at the thought of being saved. But the archdeacon lowered his eyes and led the donkey away. The red sand ran slowly, slowly through the glass.

"Water . . ."

Through the angry, cruel crowd came Esmeralda and her goat.

Silently, she took a gourd from her belt
and raised it to Quasimodo's parched lips.

"That's the gypsy girl!" exclaimed an
amazed woman.

"The one he tried to take away!"

"But still she took pity!"

"Curse to the gypsy!" cried the recluse
suddenly from the Rat-hole.

Esmeralda turned pale and stumbled through the crowd.

The flogging was over. The torturer washed Quasimodo's bleeding
shoulders, rubbed them with some ointment, and threw a yellow
cloth over him. But Quasimodo still had to endure another hour on
the pillory, while the crowd's insults rained down on him.

*Quasimodo winced
under the painful blows of
the torturer's whip.*

Inside a lady's house
Wealthy ladies were expected to greet guests warmly in their lavish homes.

Chapter five

PHOEBUS

Fleur-de-Lys scowled angrily as Phoebus flirted with Esmeralda.

WINTER TURNED INTO SPRING, and on a warm, sweet-scented day in March some wealthy ladies stood at the balcony of one of the houses in front of Notre-Dame. Captain Phoebus stood with them. One of the girls, Fleur-de-Lys, hoped to marry the captain, and her mother was working very hard to arrange this. Phoebus, though, was bored by the women until one of them noticed a gypsy dancing in the square below.

"Oh, Phoebus, doesn't the little angel dance divinely?"

Phoebus recognized the gypsy, but didn't say anything. His eyes strayed across to the cathedral; the archdeacon was also looking down at Esmeralda.

"Let's send for her and she can come and dance for us up here for a gold coin!" suggested Fleur-de-Lys.

"Oh, yes!" replied the other ladies in chorus and sent a servant down to fetch Esmeralda.

"Anyway, darling," continued Fleur-de-Lys, "weren't you telling me you rescued a gypsy from the clutches of some monster?"

"Did I?"

Phoebus remembered Esmeralda very well when she came into the room. When she saw Phoebus, she blushed deep crimson. Djali, the goat, ran playfully through the ladies crowding around Esmeralda.

"Remember me, little one?" Phoebus asked Esmeralda.

"Yes," said Esmeralda, looking down at the floor. That one word carried one thousand hidden feelings.

"Come, child," interrupted Fleur-de-Lys. "We do not pay you to talk! Dance for us!"

"I still don't know your name, princess," continued Phoebus.

"Esmeralda."

Fleur-de-Lys felt her blood burn with jealousy and she clapped her hands for Esmeralda to start dancing. Meanwhile, in the far corner of the room, a little girl emptied some little blocks with letters on them from a pouch around Djali's neck. The goat played with them until he made the word "PHOEBUS."

Fleur-de-Lys gasped when she saw. "The goat is bewitched! The girl is a sorceress!" she cried, collapsing in a heap.

Esmeralda gathered up the little blocks, and fled down the stairs with Djali.

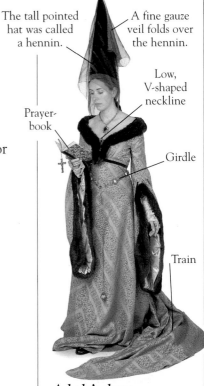

The tall pointed hat was called a hennin.

A fine gauze veil folds over the hennin.

Low, V-shaped neckline

Prayer-book

Girdle

Train

A lady's dress
Wealthy women wore gowns with a high waist, low-cut neckline, and a long train.

Courting the lady
Marriages were arranged by a girl's family. During the courtship, a chaperone made sure the couple behaved well when they met in private.

Phoebus
Phoebus means "sun." This was another name given to the handsome Greek sun god, Apollo.

Frollo gazed up at the curious sight of Gringoire balancing a cat on a wooden stool between his teeth.

Phoebus smiled at the idea of teaching the goat how to spell his name. He put on his cloak and followed Esmeralda down to the street.

Meanwhile, on the other side of the square, Claude Frollo had climbed to the top of the north tower of Notre-Dame to get a better look at Esmeralda dancing below. As soon as he saw her reappear from Fleur-de-Lys's house, he flew down the candlelit spiral staircase, his dark cape fluttering behind him. Passing the bell tower, he glimpsed Quasimodo staring down at Esmeralda between the vast silent bells. He was surprised to see Quasimodo there. Could a hunchback fall in love? Frollo wondered. Surely, he cared only for his bells . . .

When Frollo came out into the cathedral square, Esmeralda was not there. Black clouds passed over his heart. In her place stood a performer dressed in red and yellow. He was balancing a stool between his teeth, and on it there stood a large orange cat. When the cat saw the look in the priest's eyes she was so frightened she jumped off and ran away. The stool landed heavily on the performer's toe and with a cry he fell on Esmeralda's carpet. A small crowd moved away without throwing him any coins. Then the priest recognized the performer as the poet Gringoire.

"Gringoire! What are you doing?"

"Claude Frollo! How good to see you!" replied Gringoire. "This is easier than writing poems, and it gives me time to be with Esmeralda."

Frollo's eyes darkened.

"You know her?"

"Know her? I'm married to her!"

"What?!"

Frollo felt the ground vanish beneath his feet.

"Oh, yes. She saved me from hanging, you

know, by agreeing to marry me. But she won't let me even kiss her."

"No?"

"Never. She doesn't allow me anywhere near her. There's a talisman around her neck that she says will stop her from loving any man until she finds her mother. She was separated from her as a young baby, you see, but . . ."

"Go on!"

Frollo's eyes fixed onto Gringoire's every word.

"Well, Frollo, I believe she loves another."

"Who?!"

"Sometimes I catch her whispering his name. Her little goat has learned to spell it. P-H-O-E-B-U-S."

"Phoebus?!"

"Yes, Captain Phoebus, the captain of the king's bodyguard. Do you know him? Frollo?" called Gringoire, but the priest had stormed back inside the cathedral.

Then Gringoire felt the pain in his toe.

Lucky talisman
Esmeralda's talisman was her own particular version of an ancient custom. People all over the world have long kept talismans to protect them from evil spirits or to bring luck.

This Native American pouch may have been used to carry bones or roots known for their healing power.

Street entertainment
Performers such as acrobats, animal performers, and musicians made a humble living by entertaining on the streets of Paris. They livened up street fairs, weddings, and religious feasts.

Tightrope walker

Pipes made music.

While one hand worked the bellows to blow air into the pipes, the other played the keys of this portable organ.

Balancing acrobats were popular entertainers at medieval festivals.

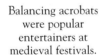

The hurdy-gurdy player turned the handle and played the keys at the same time.

Flageolet player

Juggling to music

Hurdy-gurdy

Animals were trained to do tricks such as walking on stilts.

Jehan begged Frollo for money for his studies.

Life's work
Frollo spent many hours in his cell studying an early form of chemistry called alchemy. He was trying to find ways to make gold and to live forever. Some people thought this was witchcraft.

Gold

Secret symbols used by alchemists

University scholars
At the age of sixteen, wealthy boys went to university colleges, where they lived and studied in hotels or boarding houses.

Students studied theology, law, medicine, or the arts.

Chapter six

SECRET RENDEZVOUS

LATE ONE AFTERNOON, A LOUD KNOCK on the door disturbed Claude Frollo in his cell crowded with magic books and dusty globes in the north tower of Notre-Dame. It was his brother Jehan calling to borrow money, as he often did.

"Come in!" called Frollo.

Jehan entered, nervously eyeing the seven bat skulls on the windowsill. "Dear brother, I am sorry to . . . um, disturb you, but I need to borrow a little money . . . for my studies."

Claude Frollo knew his brother only too well. "Are you sure it is not to spend on red wine in the tavern?"

"Well, if there is a little left over after buying my books I may have a small glass with my friend Phoebus."

"Who?!"

"Oh, Captain Phoebus, a gentleman. I am meeting him tonight before his meeting with a young lady called Esmeralda."

The priest frowned. He had spoiled his little brother ever since their parents had died. But suddenly his generosity snapped. "You've had enough from me," he growled. "Be gone."

Jehan bid his brother farewell, stealing his wallet as he went. Frollo didn't notice because his mind was elsewhere.

Frollo reached for his dark cape, blew out the candles, and followed Jehan. A small silver dagger was already in his pocket.

When Jehan met Phoebus in a tavern, Frollo hid in a doorway until they came out again.

"Have fun with the girl, Phoebus!" called Jehan, tripping on the cobbled stones.

Phoebus went on his way. As he walked, he noticed a shadow creeping along the walls behind him.

"Who's there?" he called.

Claude Frollo, his face hidden, stepped out of the shadows. Phoebus drew his sword. It glistened in the moonlight.

"What do you want?"

"Merely to know if you are seeing the gypsy tonight."

"What business is it of yours, stranger?"

"If you are meeting her, prove it, and I will give you a bag of gold coins," said the hooded man.

Student life
Like many of his fellow students, Jehan did not take life too seriously. Money that should have been spent on books was often spent on wine at the tavern.

A hooded stranger came up behind Phoebus.

St.-Michel Bridge
Paris's four bridges all had houses on them. On the St.-Michel Bridge, tapestry-makers, dyers, and second-hand-clothing traders sold their wares.

Iron disks at both ends of the grip protect the hands.

Dangerous weapon
Daggers were used to wound opponents at close range. Although illegal, they were often carried for personal protection.

Sharp blade was encased in leather sheath.

The night watchmen
Each district of Paris had its own night watchmen, a group of wealthy citizens who took turns patrolling the streets, like police.

"Very well," said Phoebus, "follow me."

The hooded man followed the captain to a house on the St.-Michel Bridge.

"Come inside with me," said Phoebus, "and you can watch from the room next door. You will see all for a bag of gold coins!"

Frollo hid himself in the dark room. After a little while, he heard Esmeralda and Phoebus walk into the room next door. Through a wide crack in the door of his hiding place, Frollo saw the captain undo her cape. Phoebus placed it gently down on the edge of the bed and took Esmeralda in his arms.

"Oh, Phoebus, I have dreamed of such a moment for so long!" whispered Esmeralda into his ear. "Tell me you love me . . ."

Each word tortured Frollo.

"Of course, my precious. Later . . ." Phoebus told Esmeralda. He began to undo the talisman around her neck.

"Stop, darling! You mustn't! That is to help me find my mother!" cried Esmeralda.

Her eyes shone in the darkness of the room.

"So you do not love me?" protested Phoebus, his head swimming with wine.

"Oh, yes, yes!" said Esmeralda.

She put her soft, pretty arms around his neck and he drew her to him. They kissed.

Frollo could not bear to watch.

"I love you, Phoebus, I love you," whispered Esmeralda. She looked up into the captain's eyes but there, instead, she saw the dark, terrifying eyes of another man who held in his hands a gleaming dagger.

Phoebus felt Esmeralda shudder. He turned, and the dagger came down swiftly toward his heart. Esmeralda screamed. Then she felt

A man with dark eyes threatened Phoebus with a dagger.

a chilling kiss and fainted.

When Esmeralda woke up, the room was filled with night watchmen. A woman stood by the blood-soaked body of Phoebus, saying, "I heard a scream and ran up the stairs as fast as my legs would carry me and there he was and there she was and there was the dagger between them!"

"Oh, Phoebus," whispered Esmeralda.

The soldiers tied her hands together with thick ropes, and led her down the stairs.

The man with the dark eyes was gone.

WITCHCRAFT
Esmeralda had trained her goat to do tricks, but such tricks were seen as witchcraft.

Unfair death
People thought those who had "magical" powers were witches. Since it was impossible to prove them guilty, courts often sentenced "witches" to death unfairly. Most were burned at the stake in public squares.

Guilty termites
Animals were often put on trial for crimes, including witchcraft. In one case, termites were found guilty of eating through the leg of a French bishop's chair, which had made him fall over and badly knock his head.

Chapter seven

A BROKEN HEART

L EAVES BLEW ACROSS THE SQUARE outside the Palace of Justice, where a few old women had gathered to talk.

"They say a gypsy is being tried today for the murder of a soldier!"

"I've heard she's a witch and that her goat can speak to the devil!"

Inside, Esmeralda sat. Speechless. Tearless. Her one thought was for Phoebus.

A witness spoke, "There were two men – a handsome captain and another man in black, whose face was hidden by a dark hood. All of a sudden, I heard a cry from upstairs and something falling to the floor. Then a black shadow went past the window. I called the night watchmen and we went upstairs, where the gypsy lay pretending to be dead."

"Bring in the second accused," bellowed the judge. In came Esmeralda's goat.

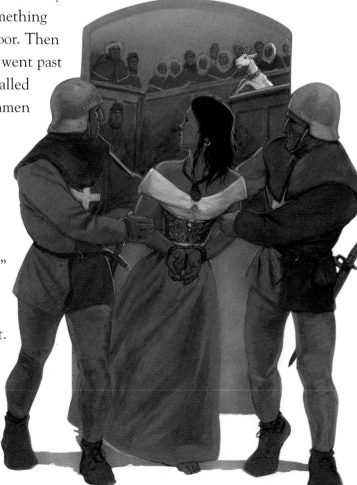

Esmeralda was led to the torture chamber.

A court official held out Esmeralda's tambourine and asked the goat, "What time is it?"

The goat tapped the tambourine seven times, just as the bells of Notre-Dame struck seven.

Next, a set of letters was emptied out onto the floor, and Djali picked out the name "Phoebus."

"This goat is possessed!" declared the judge. He turned to Esmeralda. "You are accused of using witchcraft to kill Captain Phoebus with the help of this goat."

"I am innocent. I love Phoebus," said Esmeralda.

"Phoebus is dead. Did you kill him?"

She paled. "No! A priest! A priest is following me!"

The judge became restless. "Very well! To the torture chamber! You'll change your mind!"

She was dragged along dark corridors to a room filled with iron torture instruments. A clerk sat in a corner, ready to take notes. By the fire, a bearded man prepared red-hot coals with rusty tongs. The torturers made Esmeralda lie down on a leather bed.

"They say you dance, so we'll begin with your feet!" they said.

"Mercy!" screamed Esmeralda.

"No more dancing for you!"

"Say you killed him!" said one of the torturers.

"Oh, Phoebus," whispered Esmeralda.

"Say it!"

"Yes, yes!" cried Esmeralda.

"And you are a witch?"

"Yes," moaned Esmeralda softly.

The guards led her hobbling back to the courtroom. Djali's heartbroken bleating filled the air with sorrow.

"So, you've changed your mind!" exclaimed the judge. "Good! In two days you will pray for the forgiveness of your soul outside the great door of Notre-Dame."

Esmeralda hid her face in her hands.

"Then you shall be taken to the *Place de Grève* to be hanged. Your goat shall hang with you. May God have mercy on your soul."

The clerk wrote down what was said in the torture chamber.

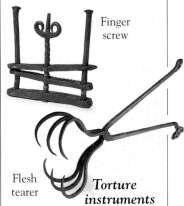
QUESTION TORTURE
Prisoners were taken to a room outside the courtroom, and tortured to make them confess to their crimes.

Finger screw

Flesh tearer

Torture instruments
Torturers' methods included squeezing prisoners' fingers or feet in metal screws, and tearing bits of flesh off with the flesh tearer.

Pressing
Those who refused to plead "guilty" or "not guilty" were "pressed." Weights were placed on top of their body until they gave in.

Palace dungeon
In a round tower, under the Palace of Justice's water reservoir, was the dungeon. Its cells were cold and damp, with only straw or bare stones for prisoners to sleep on.

Solitary confinement
To stop them from escaping, prisoners were kept manacled to their cell walls.

Sturdy iron manacles went around the wrist, ankle, or neck.

Visiting the prisoner
Prisoners' only contacts with the outside world were members of the clergy, such as priest or nuns, and the jailer.

Esmeralda lay shivering in the darkness of the dungeon, not knowing if it was night or day. Djali slept at her feet next to the tambourine, now broken. Drops of rainwater from a crack in the ceiling fell upon her tear-stained face. "Phoebus …" she whispered in the dark for the thousandth time.

The door opened, letting in a shaft of blinding light from the world outside, then closed.

"Who's there?"

A shadow fell before her, darker than other shadows. It spoke.

"Are you ready?"

She felt a cold sickening. That voice.

"Ready for what?"

"Ready to die."

Esmeralda clenched her pale, thin fingers. It was him.

"You! Why have you done this?" she asked.

"Because I love you!" exclaimed Frollo.

His hot words fell upon her like sharp ice.

"But I hate you! Why do I deserve such love?"

A drop of cold water fell upon her cheek.

"From the day I saw you dance in the square in that pretty dress I have thought only of you. I tried to study but your beauty returned to haunt me. Yes, I love you. I tried once to steal you. Return my love and you will be free!"

"I would rather hang."

"Say you love me!"

"Never! . . . I love Phoebus."

"Phoebus is dead. My dagger touched his heart!"

"Oh, I am as cold as winter without his love," she wept.

"My love would turn your winter into spring!"

Esmeralda shuddered. "I would rather die!" she said.

"Then die!" Shaking, Frollo left the dungeon, and walked to the *Place de Grève*. Passing the Rat-hole, the recluse called out to him:

"Good sir, you are a man of God. Please find my daughter."

"No!"

"Oh, how I hate gypsies!"

"Madam, they hang one soon."

"They do? Oh, there is one I hate above all others. She is terribly pretty, about the age my sweet daughter would be, and she dances like an angel!"

Her words were daggers entering his dark heart.

"Lady, she will dance no more! She's the one they hang!" he said, walking swiftly toward Notre-Dame.

In the corner of her dark cell, the recluse kissed her little pink shoe.

"Oh shoe, where is your foot?" she moaned softly.

Like Esmeralda, she wept alone.

Basic fare
Prisoners were fed bread and water, but they could receive food or money from convents or charitable people via the jailer.

Esmeralda shrank back with horror when Frollo begged her to love him.

Chapter eight

THE DEATH CART

CAPTAIN PHOEBUS WAS NOT DEAD. The priest's silver dagger had narrowly missed his heart and for some weeks he rested in a boring garrison town west of Paris. But he grew stronger with the coming of spring and once again yearned for the company of women.

So one fine afternoon he rode into Paris and found himself at the house of the fair Fleur-de-Lys on the square in front of Notre-Dame.

"Phoebus, darling! Where have you been?" she exclaimed as he was shown onto her balcony.

"Dreaming of you, my love!" he lied.

Her hair was adorned

Esmeralda looked up and saw her beloved Phoebus.

DEATH CART
Once found guilty, prisoners were taken by wagon to Notre-Dame. There, they confessed their crime and asked God for forgiveness before being taken to the Grève to be hanged.

Processional cross
The cross, symbol of Christianity, was carried at the head of many kinds of processions.

with sweet-scented roses, and as she kissed him warmly, he easily forgot the passion of the gypsy girl.

She noticed his bandaged chest.

"What is this?" she said, turning pale.

"Oh, I fell off a wild horse on some distant plain!"

Phoebus kissed away any further questions.

He took her hand and led her behind the curtains. She stopped, smiling.

"But Phoebus, what if my mother should walk in?"

He put his arms around her slender waist.

"Oh, Phoebus, tell me you love only me and that we will be married soon!"

"Of course."

The bells of Notre-Dame chimed and Fleur-de-Lys remembered.

"Oh, I believe they're hanging a little witch and her goat today. Don't let it spoil this moment for us."

The captain cradled her in his arms. They both looked down onto the sunlit square below.

Below, Esmeralda sat looking pale in the fatal cart as it rattled toward Notre-Dame's great doors. The doors opened, and the sound of chanting filled the air. It was the Mass for the Dead.

Holding a cross, Frollo waited at the door of Notre-Dame. Esmeralda was taken down from the cart, her hands untied.

"My child, have you asked God's forgiveness for your sins?" the archdeacon asked, pressing a lighted candle into her hands.

"Demon!"

"It is not too late! Say you love me!" Frollo whispered.

"I hate you!"

He walked away mouthing a prayer, and the executioner's attendants retied Esmeralda's hands. A thick rope already hung around her neck. Esmeralda looked up to the sky. Then she saw Captain Phoebus alive upon a distant balcony with his arms around a beautiful young lady.

"Oh, Phoebus! Phoebus!"

She tried to reach out to him, but her arms were tied. "Phoebus!"

He did not hear her cry.

Fleur-de-Lys and Phoebus watched from above.

Blessed taper
Condemned prisoners were given a wax candle, symbolizing the light of their soul.

Up above, among the vast statues of Notre-Dame's Gallery of the Kings, Quasimodo watched the sad scene below. No one noticed his strange figure there, for his deformed and outstretched face could have been confused with any one of the stone monsters. Only his half-red, half-mauve tunic made him stand out from the Gallery.

A crow flapped its black wings above his huge head, then flew downward toward Esmeralda. Quasimodo wanted to be able to fly to her like the birds. But how could he?

"Hang the witch!" cried the crowd below.

There was so little time! Quasimodo found a vast coil of rope and tied it around a king's stone head. He heaved the rope over the side and watched it uncoil like a giant serpent. Like a raindrop sliding down a windowpane, Quasimodo slipped down. All eyes were fixed on Esmeralda, who was about to be taken to the *Place de Grève* to be hanged at the gibbet. The crowd did not see the hunchback sliding ever nearer to the ground.

"I love you, Phoebus," whispered Esmeralda. Now she waited silently for death.

Quasimodo slid to the bottom of the great rope.

Out of nowhere, Quasimodo swooped down from the Gallery of the Kings, and lifted Esmeralda into his arms.

Like a lion, he leaped onto the executioners, flattening them with his fists. With one hand, he lifted up the gypsy, and swung inside the cathedral.

At the door, he turned to the amazed crowd and, holding his prize aloft, bellowed one word that echoed and echoed across Paris.

"Sanctuary!"

He took her inside and bolted the door.

He ran to the bell tower and held her up to the sky.

"Sanctuary!" repeated the crowd.

Esmeralda opened her eyes and, with horror, saw Quasimodo's face. But she was safe.

Renovated Gallery of the Kings today

Gallery of the Kings
The Gallery of the Kings was lined with the 28 statues of the kings of Israel. To get to the square below, Quasimodo had to drop about 60 ft (18 m).

Twenty-one original heads remain in a Paris museum.

Long before Esmeralda's dramatic rescue, after he had blessed Esmeralda in front of Notre-Dame, Claude Frollo had hurried away from the cathedral to be alone with his thoughts. He crossed the Seine by boat, and walked along the city walls, lost deep in his dark imaginings.

"She will be dead by now," he whispered under the trees. "I have killed her!"

Better to hand her to the executioner, he thought, than to let her be gathered up in the arms of the handsome captain. But then he thought of her soft, white neck twisted by a rough rope, and the first waves of guilt swept over him.

At nightfall, he walked slowly back to the city. Under the moon, he opened the great door of Notre-Dame. Something white was moving along the gallery above. A white dress! It was her!

"Oh, God!" thought Frollo. "She has been cold only a few hours and already she walks as a ghost!"

He passed by Notre-Dame's breviary and tried to find consolation in a prayer for forgiveness. High above the arches overhead, Esmeralda returned softly to her secret room. From a distance, unseen, Quasimodo watched over her until she finally fell safely into a deep sleep.

Sanctuary!
Churches were declared places of sanctuary. Escaped prisoners could avoid their punishments if they were careful to stay inside.

Praying for forgiveness
Priests spend a lot of time praying, or "talking" to God. Christians believe that God will forgive those who are sorry for their wrong-doings and who pray to ask for guidance.

Notre-Dame of Paris

Quasimodo's home still stands in the very center of Paris, on the *Île de la Cité*, the island in the Seine River where the city was founded. Building began in 1163, and it was finished 170 years later. Dedicated to Our Lady (*Notre-Dame*), it made Paris the religious capital of France. Parisians came to worship at the cathedral, and services for religious holidays and state occasions were held there.

Notre-Dame today

Frollo's cell

Priests used small cells for study and reflection. Frollo would have worked above the Gallery of the Colonnettes, high in the north tower.

THE MEDIEVAL CATHEDRAL

In the Middle Ages in Europe, the Roman Catholic Church was central to people's lives. The cathedral served as an important center for work, prayer, and study.

The clergy said mass every Sunday.

Pilgrims

Pilgrims traveled long distances to cathedrals to pray and ask for God's blessing.

First and last rites

Soon after birth, Christians were baptized at the cathedral or local church font; when they died, a priest said a prayer for them before they were buried.

Font

Church music

People went to cathedrals to listen to music, played on instruments such as harps, organs, and flutes.

Reed flute

Learning from the clergy

Primary school lessons were held in local churches and cathedrals. Students studied Latin, grammar, arithmetic, music, and geometry.

The foundling bed

People left unwanted babies such as Quasimodo on a wooden bed on the steps of Notre-Dame. They were taken in by the clergy and given homes.

Gallery of the Colonnettes (small columns)

North tower

The south tower housed the big bell, Jacqueline.

Portal of the Virgin

At the time of the story, 11 steps led to the portals.

Portal of the Judgment

Portal of St. Anne

Curious people stopped to look at baby Quasimodo.

Gallery of the Kings

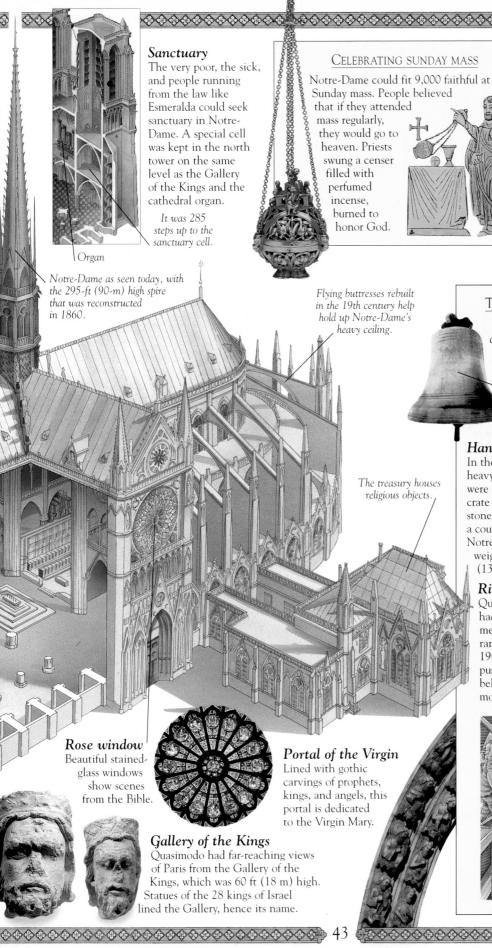

Sanctuary

The very poor, the sick, and people running from the law like Esmeralda could seek sanctuary in Notre-Dame. A special cell was kept in the north tower on the same level as the Gallery of the Kings and the cathedral organ.

It was 285 steps up to the sanctuary cell.

Organ

Notre-Dame as seen today, with the 295-ft (90-m) high spire that was reconstructed in 1860.

CELEBRATING SUNDAY MASS

Notre-Dame could fit 9,000 faithful at Sunday mass. People believed that if they attended mass regularly, they would go to heaven. Priests swung a censer filled with perfumed incense, burned to honor God.

Watchful gargoyles

Shaped like monsters, Notre-Dame's gargoyles help drain rainwater from the top of the cathedral.

Flying buttresses rebuilt in the 19th century help hold up Notre-Dame's heavy ceiling.

The treasury houses religious objects.

THE BELLS OF NOTRE-DAME

The bells of the cathedral could be heard all over Paris. Their main purpose was to communicate.

The big bell was named "Jacqueline" in 1400, and later renamed "Emmanuel."

Hanging the bell

In the Middle Ages, heavy cathedral bells were hoisted using a crate filled with heavy stones that acted as a counterweight. Notre-Dame's Jacqueline weighed 28,660 lb (13,000 kg).

Crate

Ringing the bell

Quasimodo must have had the strength of 12 men to pull the rope that rang Jacqueline. Later, in the 19th century, four pairs of men pushed down on treadles (shown below); in 1934 an electric motor replaced them.

Treadle

Rose window

Beautiful stained-glass windows show scenes from the Bible.

Portal of the Virgin

Lined with gothic carvings of prophets, kings, and angels, this portal is dedicated to the Virgin Mary.

Gallery of the Kings

Quasimodo had far-reaching views of Paris from the Gallery of the Kings, which was 60 ft (18 m) high. Statues of the 28 kings of Israel lined the Gallery, hence its name.

Chapter nine

SANCTUARY

SHAFTS OF GOLDEN morning light woke Esmeralda. She wondered if perhaps she was in heaven, before remembering her flight up the spiral stairs in the arms of the hunchback. With horror she remembered his hairy hands on her bare shoulders.

Quasimodo brought Esmeralda a surprise.

Paris rooftops
From her cell, Esmeralda looked out onto the Seine River and over the roofs of the houses on the square in front of Notre-Dame.

Yet he was the one who had saved her. She saw the checkered rooftops of Paris below. Out there somewhere breathed Phoebus and the very thought made her heart miss a beat. But that woman on the balcony? Well, perhaps that was his sister. He was alive! That was all that mattered. Esmeralda was startled to find Quasimodo watching her from the door. She shuddered as if she'd seen a large spider.

"I . . . I did not mean to startle you," he said.

"Why have you saved me?" asked Esmeralda, softly.

Even though he could not hear her words, he sensed their meaning. "Once, when I was thirsty, you gave me water. You cared for me and now I will care for you. Stay in the cathedral and you will be safe. No one must see you, so only leave your cell when it gets dark."

Quasimodo gave her a novice's habit left on the cathedral steps by some charitable ladies from the hospital next door. "Here, put this on. Don't worry, I won't harm you. You are so beautiful. I did not know how ugly I was until I saw your beauty. It is not my fault I am so ugly," he said.

He wept and his tears moved her away from her own sorrows.

Later Quasimodo returned with a surprise for her. It had white legs and golden bells.

"Oh, my little darling Djali, so you're safe, too!" cried Esmeralda.

Quasimodo grinned, and gave her a silver whistle. "Blow the whistle if you ever need me and I will run to you," Quasimodo told her. "I will be able to hear it."

Then he was gone. Esmeralda no longer felt frightened of him.

Novice's habit
Quasimodo gave Esmeralda a novice's habit to wear. A novice is someone who is training to be a nun. The nuns and novices who worked at the hospital next door to Notre-Dame wore long white habits like this one.

A few days later, Esmeralda saw Phoebus cross the square below. "Shall I get him for you?" asked Quasimodo.

Esmeralda's face blossomed, so Quasimodo bounded down the steps and ran out to meet the captain.

"What is your business, vile creature?" scoffed Phoebus.

"A lady who loves you waits for you!" replied Quasimodo.

Phoebus remembered the scene in the backstreet and drew his sword. "You have crossed my path before, monster!" he said.

"Go tell your lady I am to be married!"

Phoebus kicked the bellringer and rode off.

When she saw Quasimodo return alone, Esmeralda's heart sank. That night, she cried herself to sleep.

"Stop! A lady who loves you waits for you!" Quasimodo told Phoebus.

Celibacy

Frollo's feelings for Esmeralda made him feel very guilty, because he had promised not to marry, and vowed to love only God.

Catholic priests vow to be celebate and not to marry.

When he heard the whistle, Quasimodo came running.

Meanwhile, the archdeacon heard rumors that Esmeralda had been rescued. "So," he thought, "she was alive!" Frollo's eyes darkened at the very idea. Images of Esmeralda haunted him; he wanted to spend all his waking hours near her just like Quasimodo. Could it be that he was becoming jealous of a hunchback?

Frollo shut himself in his cell in the cloister and refused to come out for several weeks. From his window he sometimes saw Esmeralda with her goat, and sometimes with Quasimodo. He noticed how the hunchback doted on her, and this made him even more jealous.

One evening Frollo could bear it no longer. He had to see her! He found a lantern among the bat skulls in his study and opened a small drawer containing a key. He lit the lantern and tiptoed toward Esmeralda's cell.

Only the goat heard the key turn in the lock. Djali bleated in alarm and awoke Esmeralda.

"Quasimodo?" Esmeralda whispered softly. Silently, the lantern came closer. Djali shook with fear.

Then suddenly, Esmeralda felt someone try to kiss her cheek.

"No!" she yelled.

She reached out for her silver

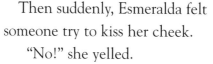

whistle and blew as hard as she could.

The next thing he knew, Frollo felt a powerful arm pulling him away from Esmeralda.

"Leave her alone!" came a voice in the dark.

Frollo could not see clearly who it was, but he heard teeth chattering with rage. The priest thought he could make out the form of Quasimodo and the shadow of a gleaming cutlass over his head. The next instant, Frollo found himself

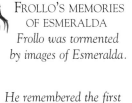

FROLLO'S MEMORIES OF ESMERALDA
Frollo was tormented by images of Esmeralda.

He remembered the first time he saw her dancing on the Place de Grève.

flat on the ground with a knee pressing against his chest. The cutlass came closer. Frollo was sure he would die.

Then, suddenly, his opponent hesitated. "There will be no blood spilled on her," he said, and dragged the priest out of the dark cell into the moonlight outside.

The moon shone on Frollo's face, and Quasimodo saw who it was. He dropped to his knees in surprise. "My lord," he said, solemnly offering the priest the cutlass, "first you will have to kill me, then you can do anything you like."

Frollo said nothing. He kicked Quasimodo aside, and disappeared into the cathedral.

He couldn't bear to think that she loved Phoebus.

He wanted Esmeralda to love him.

But if Esmeralda wouldn't love him, Frollo wanted her to die. He could not live with the idea of sharing her with either Quasimodo or Phoebus.

Frollo convinced Gringoire to muster up the outcasts to save Esmeralda from parliament.

Parliament
The Parliament of Paris was the only body that could overrule the Church's right to offer a prisoner sanctuary. With the king at its head, it met in the Palace of Justice.

Chapter ten

GRINGOIRE'S PLAN

LATE ONE GRAY AFTERNOON, Pierre Gringoire met Claude Frollo on the street.

"Frollo! It's good to see you!" cried the poet.

"Gringoire! Do you know the news about your wife?"

"Yes, Frollo. I hear the hunchback saved her. Isn't it wonderful? By the way, is the goat safe?"

"Yes!

"Oh, good, I am so fond of the little thing."

"Gringoire, listen! She is not safe in her sanctuary forever; parliament are meeting to discuss her case. Soon, time will run out. She must be rescued!"

"Oh, yes, I expect she will be."

"You must rescue her!"

"But how, Frollo?"

"Go to her. She trusts you. Change clothes with her and let her escape in your place."

"But what about me?"

"You may be lucky. Otherwise at least you'll have died saving her."

"But, Frollo, I don't really want to die. I have a happy life, performing my tricks, writing poems, drinking a little wine . . ."

"Gringoire! She saved you once. Or is your memory so short?"

The poet looked down at the cobblestones. The bells of Notre-Dame chimed and he considered death. Perhaps he would meet some great dead poets in heaven.

"She will hang, Gringoire!" insisted the archdeacon.

"Wait, Frollo! There is another way. I will go and seek the help of King Clopin and the outcasts of the Court of Miracles. He's fond of Esmeralda and they all like a good fight."

"What on earth will he do?"

Gringoire leaned across and whispered his plan. The priest nodded, then set out for Notre-Dame under darkening clouds. Gringoire, too, headed for home.

A few hours later, Gringoire stood before Clopin on his throne of straw in the Court of Miracles. The King of the Outcasts took a drink from a chipped jug of red wine and asked absent-mindedly, "What did you say, Gringoire?"

"I've already explained. Esmeralda needs us!" replied Gringoire.

"Oh, yes! The gypsy! We'll storm the cathedral, rescue her, kill a few soldiers and maybe steal some silver candlesticks. Easy!"

"When shall we do it, Clopin?" asked Gringoire eagerly.

"Tonight!" decided Clopin. "Everyone, choose a weapon!" he ordered. "We march in one hour."

Shouting with excitement, the vagabonds, thieves, and gypsies gathered around an enormous wooden chest, filled with all kinds of weapons – axes, flails, swords, crossbows, halberds, and daggers.

Then, suddenly, it was time to go.

"Silence as we cross Paris," ordered Clopin. "Don't light the torches until we reach Notre-Dame! March!"

The long black procession set off across the bridge to the Île de la Cité, striking terror into the night watchmen.

Poll-ax

Flail

Sword

Armed men
The outcasts of the Court of Miracles struck fear into the night watchmen because they were so numerous and so well-armed.

Clopin ordered the outcasts to arm themselves.

Gold treasure
Notre-Dame sparkled with priceless gold crosses, candlesticks, chandeliers, and jeweled chalices used to hold the wine at Sunday mass.

Chalice

Deadly lead
Molten lead was a common weapon in siege warfare. It was poured through pipes in castle walls onto attackers below. Gargoyles' mouths made ideal spouts for spewing out molten lead.

Repair works
Building materials from ongoing repairs were often left lying around cathedrals. From the height of the Gallery of the Kings – about 60 ft (18 m) – even the smallest piece of stone became a lethal weapon.

Airborne wood and bricks were dangerous.

Chapter eleven

STORMING NOTRE-DAME

SOMETHING KEPT QUASIMODO FROM SLEEPING. His eyes were closed, but his mind was wide awake. He went to the window. With horror, he saw shadows coming toward the cathedral from the river, and the outline of a thousand sharpened pitchforks. In no time at all a crowd flooded into the square in front of Notre-Dame. A light shone out, and instantly the square lit up with torches. They were coming for Esmeralda! He ran to her room. She was deep in sleep with Djali curled at her feet. No, he would not wake her. He ran to the Gallery of the Kings.

"Bring out the gypsy!" yelled Clopin from below. "Or we'll attack!"

Quasimodo thought they had come to kill Esmeralda. He hurled a rock down into the darkness.

"Break down the door! Smash it!" spat an enraged Clopin. "Think of the gold treasure inside! To work!"

Quasimodo gathered enough rocks to crack a hundred skulls. But it was not enough. Then, suddenly, he remembered that they had been repairing the roof of the cathedral that day. He ran up the tower and found a whole arsenal of materials: wooden beams, stones, and coils of lead. Below, the door splintered, but it did not split.

"Use your teeth if you must!" cried Clopin.

"We need a battering ram, Your Majesty!"

"Oh, and where shall we get one at midnight? A battering-ram shop?"

With superhuman strength the bellringer lifted up a wooden beam and slid it over the side of the Cathedral. Like the blade of a giant windmill, it fell. It landed on the cobblestones below, and the cries of the dying filled the night.

"What are you waiting for!" shrieked Clopin. "There's your battering ram!"

The door was breaking. There were no more rocks. Clopin was winning. Just then Quasimodo spied the coils of lead. He lit a fire with his lantern and laid the lead

on the fire. Then he watched with delight as the molten lead poured along the gutter and ran out in bright streams through the mouths of the gargoyles.

"Break down the doors!" cried Clopin, waving his whip in the air.

Dockers' ladder
Jehan got a ladder from the docks along the Seine River, near Notre-Dame. Merchants used wooden ladders to carry their goods from their boats onto the docks.

High up in the Gallery of the Kings, Quasimodo waited. Screams sounded as the hot lead landed on the outcasts below. Men scattered like sparks blown from a fire by a sudden breeze.

"Cowards!" yelled Clopin. "So you'll leave Esmeralda to the wolves? Do I fight alone?"

"No!" roared the outcasts.

Clopin looked around him.

"And where is Gringoire?"

"Sneaked off," smirked Jehan, suddenly appearing before Clopin.

Jehan laughed at Quasimodo, who was hiding behind the statue of a king.

Jehan was wearing the shining armor of a knight, complete with a frightening beaked helmet. He carried a crossbow, and behind him he was pulling a long ladder.

"Clopin," he said, "I know the best places to climb up onto the Gallery of the Kings. There's a door there that leads right inside the cathedral!"

"Jehan, tell me one thing," replied Clopin. "How many do you believe are up there?"

"I know precisely," said Jehan.

"Tell me! Twelve dozen?"

"No, one," said Jehan.

"One!" cried Clopin.

"The bellringer. That is all."

"The hunchback? Alone?" exclaimed Clopin in disbelief. "To the ladders! Off with his hunch!"

Like lizards, the outcasts crawled quickly up the ladder behind Jehan. Quasimodo hid behind the statue of a king, his eye glittering. Jehan climbed up onto the Gallery and tried the door. It was locked. Before anyone else could follow Jehan, Quasimodo sent the outcasts flying helter-skelter off the ladder.

From the far side of the Gallery Jehan aimed his bow and arrow at Quasimodo. "Now to make you blind as well as deaf, beast!" he cried.

He shot the arrow at Quasimodo's huge eye, but it landed in his arm. The hunchback plucked out the arrow like an unwanted rose-thorn. In three paces he reached Jehan, lifted him up by his left leg, and hurled him into the air over the statues of the kings. Now the hunchback heard voices all around. Captain Phoebus and his men had come to restore order. Clopin and his men fought bravely, but they were no match for the king's bodyguard. They turned and fled for their lives.

Knight's helmet
Knights wore helmets to protect their heads in battle. Some helmets were shaped like fierce monsters to help frighten enemies.

Beaked helmet

Twisted cord bow-string

Wooden flights

Bow and arrow
The crossbow was a popular medieval weapon, used both in warfare and hunting. Its sharply pointed arrows were deadly at close range.

Armor
In battle, knights were covered from head to foot in plate armor. Joints allowed the knight to move easily.

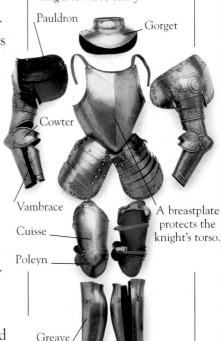

Pauldron
Gorget
Cowter
A breastplate protects the knight's torso
Vambrace
Cuisse
Poleyn
Greave
Sabaton

Inside Notre-Dame
Esmeralda passed through the cathedral's spacious side-aisles, crowned with beautiful stained-glass windows.

Red door
This side door behind the cathedral led to the old cloister courtyard.

Place de Grève   Île Notre-Dame

Escaping Notre-Dame
From the riverbank behind the cathedral, the boat rowed around the tip of the Île Notre-Dame and landed near the Place de Grève.

Chapter twelve

Escape!

WHILE QUASIMODO WAS HURLING rocks at the outcasts, Gringoire stood watching from a safe distance. A dark figure approached.

"Frollo!" cried Gringoire. "We are saving her!"

"Gringoire, this will not do! Quasimodo would rather die trying to save her than lose her. We must go and get her now!"

"But Frollo, they say she is locked in a room!"

"I have the key! Come!"

"We will never get her past these madmen!"

"There is a boat moored on the Seine at the back of the cathedral. Hurry!"

Gringoire and Frollo hurried into the cathedral up to the sanctuary cell where Esmeralda was gazing at the terrifying scene below. Like fireworks, bright molten lead flashed past the window.

"Gringoire, why are you here? What is happening?" she exclaimed.

"They are attacking the cathedral. Hurry, Esmeralda, we must save you!" cried Gringoire.

"But who is that other man?" asked Esmeralda.

"Don't worry, he's a friend," replied Gringoire.

"But why does he not speak?"

"Come on!" said Gringoire, grabbing her hand.

The two men led Esmeralda down the stairs, through the church, and out the red door into the courtyard of the cloister. They walked to the riverbank behind Notre-Dame, where a small boat was hidden among the bushes.

Gringoire held Djali close, while Esmeralda watched the other man rowing silently toward the opposite shore, his black cloak billowing like the wings of a giant bat. She shuddered.

On the other side, in front of Notre-Dame, the men-at-arms seemed to be searching for someone. Soon the distant yelling reached Esmeralda – "Witch! Death to the gypsy!" came the cries.

The rowboat reached the other shore. Gringoire tied the boat to a gnarled tree and, before Esmeralda realized what was happening, he scampered off with Djali, leaving her alone with the other man. Without speaking, the stranger took Esmeralda roughly by the hand, and led her to the *Place de Grève*.

Esmeralda shivered as she heard the cries of "Witch! Death to the gypsy!" in the distance.

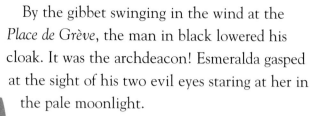

By the gibbet swinging in the wind at the *Place de Grève*, the man in black lowered his cloak. It was the archdeacon! Esmeralda gasped at the sight of his two evil eyes staring at her in the pale moonlight.

On the quay opposite, soldiers ran past with torches shouting, "The gypsy! Where's the gypsy? Kill her!"

"Esmeralda, I have saved you," said the priest. "Soon you will hang. Come with me, love me. You have no choice."

The gypsy was silent.

"Esmeralda, it is either my loving arms or that cold gibbet."

"The gibbet is kinder than you," she answered bluntly. "I love Phoebus."

"Say you love me!"

"Never!"

Frollo wept at her words. He could take no more.

"One last time. Do you love me?"

"I hate you!" screamed Esmeralda.

The priest led Esmeralda to the corner of the square by the Rat-hole, the dark home of the recluse. "Here hag, I have a gypsy for you!" he called. "Hold her tight while I fetch the captain!"

He walked away toward the approaching soldiers.

Esmeralda tried to run, but a cold iron grip held her. She looked down and there, through the bars of the Rat-hole, two thin, fleshless, wrinkled arms grasped her elbow.

"Please! Let me go! They are coming for me!"

"Never!" shrieked the woman. "You are a gypsy! Gypsies stole my daughter. They ate her. She would have been about your age, so after your hanging I may eat you!"

The soldiers were getting nearer. The pink light of the Paris

"Let go! They're coming for me!" cried Esmeralda. But the recluse held on tightly.

56

dawn made it impossible for Esmeralda to hide.
She was caught in the web of this mad spider,
who now held her tighter, closer.

"My child! They took my child! My own
sweet child! Lost!"

"I lost my mother!" replied Esmeralda,
falling to the ground, weeping. "Please let
me go . . ."

"See," continued the recluse, "Her little
pink shoe! All that's left of my sweet child!
One pink shoe!"

The pale morning light shone upon it.
Esmeralda felt a strange emotion, then
whispered, "Oh, heavens! Can it be?"

She opened the green bag around her neck
and out of it she took a little pink shoe. On
it was tied a rhyme:

When you the same shoe shall see,
Your mother will put her arms around thee.

"My little lost girl!" whispered the recluse.

The eyes of the girl and the recluse met. The
two shoes made a perfect pair.

"My daughter!"

"My mother!"

Blindly, Paquette kissed Esmeralda's fingers
through the bars of the Rat-hole.

"I must hold you in my arms! But the bars!"

She scuttled around in the darkness of her
cell, found a rock, and with sudden
strength smashed the bars and scooped
her daughter into the cell. Paquette
held her close.

Paquette held her daughter in
her arms, rocking her gently.

Short reunion
Paquette thanked God for returning her daughter, while Esmeralda begged her mother to save her from the officers who wanted to hang her for being a witch.

"My child!" screamed the recluse. "Please don't take my child!"

"Oh, mother, they have come to hang me! Save me!"

"My child! What have you done?"

"I don't know," wept Esmeralda.

Esmeralda made out Frollo's voice: "She's here! Follow me!"

"Quickly!" whispered Paquette. "Hide in the shadows!"

A group of soldiers gathered at the entrance of the cell, their boots shining, horses breathless. "Old woman, where is the gypsy?"

"I . . . don't know. She bit me . . . and ran off."

Mother and daughter's hearts beat loudly in the darkness.

"Then why are the bars of the cell broken?"

"I . . . I . . . a cart broke them . . . last month."

The women heard the men talking outside.

"Come on," said one. "She won't be here. The old hag hates gypsies."

The soldiers walked away from the cell. Another horse approached.

"Is she there?" came a voice.

"No, Captain Phoebus."

"Well, carry on the search!" ordered Phoebus, galloping away.

When she heard the name of the man she loved, Esmeralda forgot everything. "Phoebus!" she called out from the darkness.

But it was not Phoebus who heard her call.

"So there are two rats in the Rat-hole!" called a soldier. "Out you come!"

"Oh, mother, help me!" cried Esmeralda.

"Oh, my child!" shrieked Paquette, as the men dragged her, clinging to Esmeralda, out of the Rat-hole into the light of day.

Perfect pair
Esmeralda had spent her life looking for the mother who had the little pink shoe that matched hers. Paquette had kept her pink shoe as a momento of the daughter she thought was dead. They came together at last, but all too briefly.

"Sorry, lady, king's orders are king's orders. She must be hanged. Fetch the ladder!"

The soldiers prepared the gibbet for the hanging.

"But my own sweet daughter!" wailed Paquette.

"Take her up the ladder!"

The harder the soldiers pulled Esmeralda from her mother, the tighter Paquette held on.

"See! Her little pink shoe! My daughter! You can't take her!"

But mother and daughter were being pulled farther up the ladder toward the gibbet.

"Mother! Help me!"

Then with one strong kick from his big boot the executioner pulled them apart. Paquette fell off of the ladder headfirst and landed on the stone pavement. She was dead.

"Now! Put the noose on the gypsy!"

Esmeralda felt the cold rope against the soft skin of her neck. She closed her eyes.

Esmeralda's death

Montfaucon gibbet
The city's largest gibbet,
Montfaucon, *stood on a hill*
outside Paris. People were
hanged on its 16 pillars.
Those hanged in Paris were
buried in the cellar there.

Last rites
Wealthy Catholics were blessed
by a priest and buried in
single graves. Criminals, the
poor, and outcasts like
Esmeralda were buried
together in common graves.

Quasimodo searched in vain for Esmeralda. Many times he returned to her cell.

He did not understand. He was the only one with a key to her cell apart from . . . the priest! The hunchback remembered with horror the scene with Frollo and the whistle.

As dawn broke, Quasimodo saw Frollo return to Notre-Dame. With the wolflike tread of a hunter, the hunchback tracked Frollo up the stairs to the north tower.

Below, women of Paris carried jugs of morning milk across the square.

But Frollo was not watching them. Silently, the hunchback followed the direction of the priest's gaze. Then, with horror, Quasimodo saw just where Esmeralda was. On the pink horizon was a girl in white with a noose around her neck. A ladder beneath her was kicked away by a hooded executioner. Hopelessly, the hunchback watched her swinging sadly in the air.

Esmeralda was dead.

The priest laughed.

Quasimodo could not hear his laugh, but he saw it through the tears that drenched his one eye.

He pushed the archdeacon over the edge. Frollo landed on a small ledge then slid down to a gutter. He clung onto a gargoyle with outstretched fingertips. His nails scratched desperately at the stone before he slipped and fell screaming to his death.

Quasimodo looked first at Esmeralda hanging from the rope at the *Place de Grève* and then at the priest on the cobblestones below.

"Oh, the only two I have ever loved!" he sobbed.

Then he vanished from the cathedral forever.

On the night of Esmeralda's death, the executioner's men took down her body from the gibbet and took it to the cellar at *Montfaucon*.

Two years after Esmeralda's tragic death, two men went to
Montfaucon to dig up the corpse of Louis XI's barber, who had
been granted pardon by the new king, and so was allowed to
be buried in his own grave in a cemetery. Among all the
bodies, two skeletons were found locked together. Lying near
one was a little pouch decorated with green beads. The
backbone of the other was twisted and terribly crooked, but
its neck wasn't broken.

"Here's one that wasn't hanged," said one of the gravediggers.

"The second one came to lie down and die with the first,"
said the other.

When the gravediggers tried to separate the two skeletons,
they crumbled into dust and blew away, toward
the towers of Notre-Dame.

"Help!" cried Frollo.
But Quasimodo just gazed
across the Seine at Esmeralda,
hanging at the Place de Grève.

VICTOR HUGO'S IDEAS

When Victor Hugo decided to write *Notre-Dame de Paris* in 1830, he wanted to make people aware that one of France's great buildings – Notre-Dame Cathedral – needed to be preserved. He also wanted to express his sympathy for the suffering of ordinary people and their constant struggle against injustice.

Victor Hugo

VICTOR HUGO'S LIFE AND WORK

Victor Hugo (1802–85) was a well-known French poet, novelist, and playwright. He spent his first ten years abroad, and left France again in 1851 to live in exile. His novels made him famous around the world.

Writing set
When he began *The Hunchback of Notre-Dame*, Hugo bought a new bottle of ink for his writing set. He only used this one bottle of ink to finish the whole 200,000–word manuscript.

Hard-earned money
Hugo wrote to support his wife and four children. He had to finish the novel in only four-and-a-half months, or pay his publishers a large fine.

Les Misérables
Hugo's next world-famous novel, *Les Misérables* (the "down-and-outs"), came out in 1862. Set in 1815, it tells of the poor people's fight for freedom.

The hero of Les Misérables is an escaped convict struggling to lead an honest life in a cruel society. He promises to care for an orphaned street urchin named Cosette.

Arc de Triomphe

Hugo's funeral
When he died in 1885, Hugo was given a state funeral at the *Arc de Triomphe* in Paris. It was attended by two million people. He was buried with other great Frenchmen in the *Panthéon*.

Although innocent, Esmeralda was hanged.

Daily life in Paris
Hugo wanted to give a sense of what daily life was like for the various classes of people living in medieval Paris. He set the story in 1482, a relatively uneventful year in French history.

Criminal injustice
Quasimodo's torture and Esmeralda's hanging show the daily injustice of medieval Paris, where ordinary people did not get a fair trial.

Hugo wanted a democracy where all people were treated fairly.

July Revolution
As Hugo sat down to write in 1830, there was a revolution on the streets of Paris. King Charles X had tried to make France a monarchy again. People took to the streets to fight for freedom from injustice.

French tricolor flag symbolizes liberty.

Beautiful and ugly

The story shows how Hugo thought that even social outcasts like Quasimodo were important in society. Although he was ugly on the outside, Quasimodo was a kind, caring person inside. He wanted to be beautiful like Esmeralda so people would love him.

Quasimodo rescued Esmeralda and offered her sanctuary in Notre-Dame Cathedral.

Anthony Quinn and Gina Lollobrigida in the 1956 movie

Apart from Frollo, Esmeralda was the only one who cared for Quasimodo.

Glass window

Notre-Dame was built in a popular medieval art style called Gothic. Architects found new ways to build very tall walls, making lots of room for beautiful stained-glass windows.

Grotesque gargoyle

Notre-Dame has more than 1,200 sculptures. Some of the most famous are the gargoyles on the gallery between the cathedral's two towers. These were reconstructed by French architect Viollet-le-Duc in the 19th century, after Hugo's novel triggered a movement to restore Gothic buildings.

Towering spire

Viollet-le-Duc also rebuilt the spire that stands at the center of the cathedral. It is 295 ft (90 m) high.

Sir Cedric Hardwicke and Maureen O'Hara in the 1939 movie

Sealed fates

The characters' lives were determined by their role in society. As a priest, Frollo could not marry Esmeralda; neither could Phoebus, who was of a higher social class than the gypsy.

Frollo followed Esmeralda all over Paris, pleading with her to love him even though he knew that he wasn't allowed to marry her because he was a priest.

The hunchback

When this story was published in England, the title was changed from *Notre-Dame de Paris* to *The Hunchback of Notre-Dame*. This shifted the attention of the story from the cathedral to the character of the hunchback.

Charles Laughton in the 1939 movie

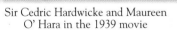

The character of the hunchback is better known than the original story, or indeed his creator, Victor Hugo.

Acknowledgments

Picture Credits

The publisher would like to thank the following for their kind permission to reproduce their photographs:

t=top, b=bottom, a=above,
c=center, l=left, r=right.

Ancient Art and Architecture: 36tl; Ronald Sheridan 43tcr.
Archives Nationale, Paris: 48bl.
Elizabeth Bacon: 41tr.
Bayerisches Landesamt für Denkmalpflege: 31tr.
Bibliothèque Nationale, Paris: 43crb.
Bodleian Library, Oxford: 9tc, 26bl, 29cr, 29bl(insert), 60bl.
Gerard Boullay Photographe, Paris: 41cr, 54tl, 54cl, 63tcb.
Bridgeman Art Library, London: Biblioteca Estene, Modena 27br; Bibliothèque Nationale, Paris 6ca, 6b, 8tl, 9tr, 16cla, 19br, 21tr, 21tc, 27cr; British Library, London 8bla, 12tl, 20cl, 29bl, 29bcr, 38tl, 42cla, 42c; Coram Foundation, London 10bl; Ecole des Beaux-Arts, Paris 19cr; Giraudon 8bca, 30bl; Musée Condé, Chantilly 7bc, 11cr, 13tr; National Gallery of Scotland, Edinburgh 42tr; Peter Willi 46cl.
British Library, London: 23tr, 35tr.
British Museum, London: 43tc, 62cl (insert).
Caisse Nationale des Monuments Historiques et des Sites, Paris: 63tr.
Jean-Loup Charmet, Paris: 32tl, 42bl, 45br, 60cl, 62cb; Musée Carnavalet 62bl, 62br.
Churches Ministry Among the Jews: 15cr.
Collections: Anne Gordon 14cl; Roger Scruton 22bl.
Cour de Cassation, Paris: 13cr.
Culver Pictures, New York: Back Jacket trb, 2tc, 43tr.
ET Archive: 8bl; Bibliothèque Nationale, Paris 6clb, 8br, 16clb.
Mary Evans Picture Library: 8ca, 36bl.
Philippe Fix, Paris: 7cr, 50bl.
Luigi Galante: 8/9c.
Giraudon, Paris: 8cla.
Ronald Grant Archive: 63tl, 63cl, 63br.
Sonia Halliday Photographs: 1c, 12bl, 29br, 42tl, 42clb, 43bcl.
Robert Harding Picture Library: Robert Cundy 63cr.
Photo Réunion des Musées Nationaux, Paris: 41trb, 42br, 43bl; Ojeda-El Majd 8clb.
Photothèque des Musées de la Ville de Paris: Back Jacket Flap tl, 6tr, 9bc, 62tl, 62cl.
Mansell Collection: 6c.
Musée de L'Armée, Paris: 16bl.
Museum of London: 37tr.
Museum of the Order of St. John: 50tl.
The Natural History Museum, London: 34bl.
Scala, Florence: 12tc; Pinacoteca Vaticano 9c.
Victoria and Albert Museum, London: 38cl.
Roger Viollet, Paris: 6cl, 9crb, 32bl.
Wallace Collection: 32cl, 49tr, 53tr, 53cr.
Warwick Castle: 53br.
Werner Forman Archive: University Museum, University of Alaska 29tr.
Janine Wiedel Photolibrary: 15tr.

Additional illustrations: Luigi Gallante; Julian Baker; Sally Alane Reason; John Woodcock; Stephen Raw.
Additional photography: Andy Crawford and Gary Ombler at the DK Photographic Studio; Norman Hollands; Sam Scott-Hunter; Richard Leaney; Alex Wilson; Victoria Hall.

DK would particularly like to thank the following people:

Angels & Bermans, London; Bridgeman Art Library; ET Archive; Mary Evans Picture Library; Éditions Gallimard/Guides Gallimard, Paris; Victoria Hall for research assistance; Joanna Hartley; Michael Homans; The London Dungeon; Yves Ozanam, Paris; Lorenzo Scaretti and Tino; Sister Mary John, The Priory of Our Lady, Hassocks; The Ringing World Ltd.; The Verger, Southwark Cathedral; Regie Singer and Eric Sutter, Société Française de Campanologie, Paris; Whitechapel Bell Foundry, London; Father Shaun Lennard; Marion Dent for proofreading.

Model: Jane Thomas.